THE ART of Fencing

My sincere thanks to the following people for their time, information, images and enthusiasm for this book:

Peter Westbrook, Director at the Peter Westbrook Foundation for Fencing in New York City, USA;

Erinn Smart, 2008 Beijing Olympic Silver Medalist, based at the Peter Westbrook Foundation for Fencing in New York City, USA;

Keeth Smart, 2008 Beijing Olympic Silver Medalist, based at the Peter Westbrook Foundation for Fencing in New York City, USA;

Paul Crook, Founder of the Chevaliers Fencing Club in Brisbane, Queensland, Australia.

Dear Reader

When I first asked students about their favourite topics, one topic mentioned was, "Swordplay, just like in the movies!"

That's how I came up with the idea for a book about fencing – a sport with swords!

FENCING IS A SPORT, BUT IT'S ALSO AN ART – THAT'S WHY THIS BOOK IS CALLED *THE ART OF FENCING*.

In this book you'll meet fencing students from four to 15 years old. In class, they imagine they're buccaneers and musketeers!

You'll also meet a brother and sister who won silver medals for fencing at the 2008 Beijing Olympic Games.

I hope you enjoy reading about the art and sport of fencing as much as I enjoyed writing this book.

Sharon Parsons

Contents

THE ART of Fencing

Page 16
TEXT TYPE
Response

1 The History of Fencing

From **Italy** to **France**

Think of knights in battle! Think of men fencing in duels! That happened hundreds of years ago when fencing was a form of attack and defence.

Today, fencing isn't like that unless you're acting as a musketeer in a play! It is a sport played and enjoyed by many people all around the world.

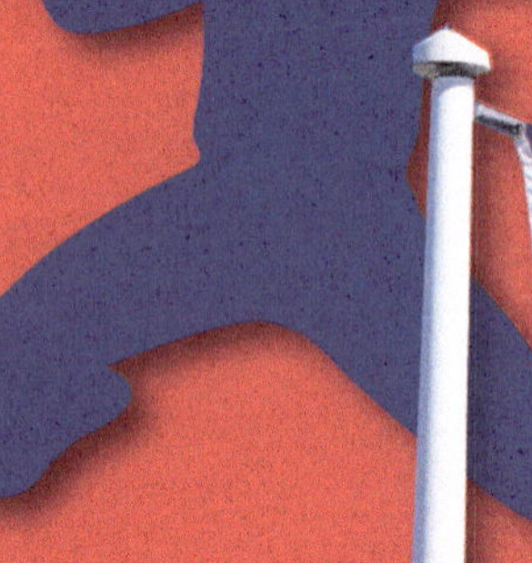

the flag of France

Fencing Secrets

In the days of fencing duels, teachers told their fencers to keep their lessons secret. Fencing secrets gave them an advantage over their opponents.

Today, fencing teachers like to keep their lessons secret, too. They want their students to win fencing competitions so ... sshhh ... keep those fencing secrets ... secret!

a fencing bout

Fencing in France

Over 500 years ago, the queen of France asked Italian fencers to teach fencing in France. Then the French invented better weapons and equipment to make fencing a safer sport. Their rules are now used at fencing clubs and in competitions.

FRANCE

2 The Art of Fencing

From **Design** to **Drama**

At school, you study arts subjects such as art and design, movement, drama and technology.

The sport of fencing is an art too. It involves:

- design of weapons and equipment
- movement that is fast and planned
- technology
- and … lots of drama!

Design in Fencing

Fencing equipment and weapons are designed to fit the person and to suit the style of fencing.

Chapter 3 explains more about design.

Technology in Fencing

In fencing competitions, electronic technology helps the judges to score points accurately.

Chapter 4 explains scoring technology.

Drama in Fencing

For young students, fencing teachers use drama or plays to teach fencing.

The students can pretend to be pirates or musketeers!

Chapter 5 shows how kids can learn fencing.

Q&A

Q: What colour are fencing uniforms?

A: Fencing uniforms are usually white – instructors can wear black.

Q: What do high-level fencers wear?

A: They usually wear a heavier jacket than other fencers. It is made with plastic foam to give the fencer extra protection.

Fencing in **Novels** and Movies

Many novels that include fencing have been made into movies. For movies, a director will work with the actors on how to fence dramatically. In some movies, actors make big, swashbuckling movements to create more drama.

Page 15 has a reference to a famous novel about fencing that has been made into many movies.

Movement in Fencing

Fencers must get into a rhythm. They work out the best positions to move to so that they can outsmart their opponents and win points. They need to be fit so that they can move with speed and skill.

Chapter 4 explains more about movement.

Fencing Weapons and Equipment

Swords and Safety

Safety First!

Fence with an experienced fencing teacher!

In fencing, there are three kinds of swords:

Épée

The épée (say "ay-pay") is a thrusting sword. Compare it to the foil, and it is heavier, has a larger guard and a stiffer blade.

Foil

The foil is also a thrusting sword. Its blade is a rectangular shape and bends more easily than an épée.

Sabre

The sabre is called a cutting sword, but fencers do not cut with it. It is similar in weight and length to the foil.

History

Where Were the Épée and Foil Designed?

The épée and the foil were first designed in France.

History and Technology

Where was the Sabre Sword Designed?

In Italy in the late nineteenth century, the heavy sabre was re-designed to make it lighter for fencing. The sabre sword was derived from a Hungarian cavalry sword.

Sword Parts

Point – Foil and Épée

The end of the sword that must touch the opponent's target area (not the head) to score points in a fencing bout.

Blade – Sabre

The point and the blade can touch the opponent from the waist, up to the head.

Guard

This protects the fencer's hand.

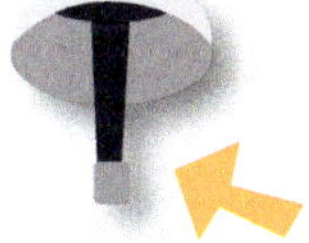

Hilt

The handle or "grip".

Safety Equipment

Mask

The mask protects the fencer's head. Its mesh visor allows fencers to see their opponents.

Bib

A thick, padded bib on the mask protects the fencer's throat.

Chest Guard

The thick padded vest protects the fencer's chest.

Gloves

Every fencer wears washable gloves. Most gloves are made from suede.

4 Fencing Bouts

Ready, **Fence**, **Halt**, Score!

Safety First!

Fencing bouts need experienced fencing supervision at all times!

In competitions, fencing bouts take place on a long, narrow strip that is about 14 metres long by two metres wide.

READY

Fencers start by standing at the "on guard" lines, an equal distance from the middle of the strip.

FENCE

The director (or referee) calls out, "Ready? Fence!" The fencers then begin by moving forward and backward quickly.

HALT

When a fencer scores a "touch", or a point, the director calls out, "Halt!" The fencers stop and the director confirms who won the point.

Technology

Electronic Scoring

Because fencing is so fast, electronic scoring helps the director. The fencer's uniform is wired so that whenever it is touched, hit points are recorded.

A lame (say "la-may") is worn over the fencer's jacket to help send electronic messages to the judges' screens.

A cord is attached to the weapon, which goes along the sleeve, down the fencer's back and ends at the scoring box.

an electronic scoreboard

Fencing Points

Each type of fencing weapon records electronic points differently.

Foil: Touches or points can be scored when the opponent is touched on the torso by the tip of the foil.

Épée: Touches or points can be scored when the opponent is touched anywhere on the body by the tip of the épée blade. Double hits are allowed so you can get double points!

Sabre: The electronic scoring aid is on the tip and the edge of the sabre blade. Touches or points can be scored when the opponent is touched anywhere above the waist by the tip or the edge of the blade.

Halt!

a fencing bout

THE WINNERS

In first-round bouts, the winner is the first fencer to get five points.

In final-round bouts, the winner is the first fencer to get 15 points.

5 Fencing for Kids

Learn from a Fencing Teacher

Paul Crook loves fencing, and so do his three young sons. He teaches boys and girls fencing in Brisbane, Queensland, Australia. The youngest are called Buccaneers and the older students are called Musketeers!

Paul Crook with his fencing students

Safety Rules

In fencing it's always safety first, with rules such as:

- the point of the weapon must touch the ground when it is not being used for fencing
- fencers must wear their safety gear (mask, jacket and gloves)
- students must stop at once when Paul calls out, "Halt!"

Fair Play in Fencing

Fair play is important. At the start of each lesson, students stand in a line and salute each other with their swords. This is a fencing tradition. It shows courtesy and respect for one another.

Paul reminds the students of the rules of fair play and safety. Then it's time for fencing fun.

History

Who Were the Buccaneers?

Hundreds of years ago, buccaneers were settlers and adventurers, mostly from France and England.

France and England were often at war with Spain. They also attacked Spanish ships. At that time buccaneers were also called pirates.

Warm-Up Exercises

As a class, the students do many warm-up exercises to improve their fencing skills:

- flexibility – by stretching leg muscles
- movement – by lunging and doing squats
- balance – by balancing the sword tip on one toe and on one finger
- hand-eye coordination – by swinging the sword like a pendulum.

flexibility

lunging

sword balance on finger

sword balance on foot

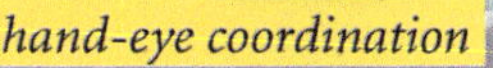

hand-eye coordination

squats

Fencing Games

Buccaneer Fencers

At Paul's fencing school, buccaneers are four to seven years old. They learn fencing skills and rules in many fun games.

A Buccaneers Fencing Game

In the pirate game, six students line up in a row. Then Paul tells the "pirates" to close their eyes while he quietly taps the shoulder of one pirate. That pirate becomes Blackbeard. The pirates open their eyes and begin "fencing". The winner is the pirate who touches Blackbeard with the point of their fencing weapon.

A team of three pirates wait with their eyes closed, while Paul decides who will be "Blackbeard".

The pirate game begins.

The pirate battle continues.

The winning pirate bows after tapping Blackbeard with his fencing weapon.

Drama and Sport

Three Billy Goats Gruff Game

One popular game is based on The Three Billy Goats Gruff. The students have to win a fencing bout against the troll on a make-believe bridge. They use their swords – not horns! The winner is the fencer who defeats the troll to get to the grass on the other side.

Musketeer Fencers

Musketeers are eight to 15 years old. At the start of each lesson, they warm up with games such as "Get the Dog a Bone". Students run around touching "bones" with their hands. Running and rapid changes in direction teach fencers to think and move quickly.

Musketeers learn more advanced fencing skills to improve their:

- balance
- footwork
- concentration
- mobility
- fitness.

Two "musketeers" are in a combat scene while a student umpires.

A Three Musketeers Fencing Game

Students are given characters from *The Three Musketeers* story and they act out fencing scenes.

Quiz

Who said, "All for one, and one for all!"

QUIZ ANSWER: SEE PAGE 16 FOR THE ANSWER.

Matt **Reviews** a **Fencing** Match

My name is Matt. I am learning to be a fencer. My teacher's name is Paul and he enjoys fencing. His love of fencing has made my brothers and me interested in the sport as well. One evening we went to watch a fencing match between a couple of people in Paul's fencing club.

A Fantastic Fencing Bout

When we arrived at the recreation centre there were many people of all ages there. Some of them were Paul's other students. Some others had never seen a fencing competition before. The two opponents were friends of Paul's, Chris and Maddy. Paul told me that they had both been fencing for over ten years!

The bout began with both fencers facing each other at the on guard lines. They were equal distance from each other until the director called out, "Fence!" Chris and Maddy moved towards one another with speed and began many exciting moves. The scores were close throughout the match until Maddy managed to win the last point.

An Exciting TIme

It was a great bout to watch. I enjoyed watching it and can't wait to go to another one. I also can't wait to go to Paul's next class to practise some of the moves.

History Feature

Fencing at the Olympic Games

Fencing for men was one of the few sports at the first modern summer Olympic Games in April 1896 in Athens, Greece.

Fencing Weapons

Only two fencing weapons were used in 1896 – the foil and the sabre.

foil

sabre

Four years later, in 1900, the épée was added to Olympic fencing competitions.

épée

Fencing for Women

Women first entered Olympic Games fencing competitions in 1924. But they were only allowed to compete with the foil.

At the 1996 Atlanta Olympic Games, women were able to fence with the épée. In 2004, women began competing in sabre fencing.

History and Sport

Wheelchair Fencing Champions

Two Australian athletes, Daphne Ceeney and Frank Ponta, won medals for fencing with foils at the 1964 Tokyo Paralympics. But it didn't stop there. Between them, they won gold, silver and bronze medals in archery, athletics and swimming in several Paralympic Games.

the Australian flag

6 Fencing in New York

A **Fencer** and a **Teacher!**

Peter Westbrook is a fencing teacher in New York City, USA. His fencing story started when he was just 13 years old.

Peter Westbrook (right) with Olympian fencer, Aki Spencer-El, who was trained at Westbrook's fencing school.

A Family Tradition

Peter's mother was Japanese. Hundreds of years ago, there were sword-fighting samurai in her family in Japan. She wanted Peter to continue the family tradition. But he couldn't be a samurai in New York! So Peter's mother arranged for him to learn the art of sword combat in the safe sport of fencing.

SAMURAI

Samurai is the name given to a Japanese warrior. There are still samurai today. In the Japanese language, samurai means "to serve". Samurai are taught rules of respect in combat.

Peter Westbrook's mother

Peter at Age 13

Peter said he did not want to learn fencing because it was not popular in New York City. So his mother paid him five dollars to go to his first lesson!

Peter learnt fencing skills quickly … and he was hooked!

Training was hard work, but he was successful.

Peter's Fencing Coach

Peter's first fencing coach was Hungarian. Peter described him as having "eyebrows like Dracula!"

Peter didn't have money to pay the coach. But he was such a good fencer, his coach taught him for free.

Peter at the 1984 Olympic Games in Los Angeles

Peter's First Olympic Games

At the 1976 Olympic Games in Montreal, Canada, Peter injured his left ankle. He could only compete on his right leg. But Peter still finished in thirteenth place – a great effort!

Peter's First Olympic Medal

At the 1984 Olympic Games in Los Angeles, USA, Peter won a bronze medal in the sabre competition. It was the first time the USA had won a fencing medal – and it would be another 20 years before they won another one!

History and Sport

Fencing Firsts

Peter Westbrook was:

- *the first African American-Japanese boy to learn fencing*
- *the first African American-Japanese person selected for the USA Olympic Fencing team in 1976*
- *the first person from the USA to win an Olympic fencing medal.*

Peter the Fencing Teacher

Since 1991, Peter has had continued success with the Peter Westbrook Foundation for Fencing in New York City.

Many people donate money to help his students learn fencing for free. Peter's fencing students also attend literacy classes at the foundation.

Peter's students learn how to lunge. Usually there are 150 kids in each class!

> FENCING HERE IN NYC HAS CHANGED THOUSANDS OF KIDS' LIVES!
>
> PETER WESTBROOK

Peter (bottom centre) with the USA fencing team in 2008

Successful Fencing Students

Many of Peter's fencing students earn scholarships to universities. Many also qualify for the Olympic Games and world fencing championships.

7 An NLD News Review

Brother and **Sister** Fencers **Win** Medals

Erinn and Keeth "bite" the silver medals that they won at the 2008 Beijing Olympic Games. Erinn won her medal with the foil and Keeth won his with the sabre.

A WIN FOR WOMEN'S FOIL

The women's foil team from the USA – of Erinn Smart, Emily Cross and Hanna Thompson – won the silver medal at the 2008 Beijing Olympics. They played in the finals against Russia with a score of 28 to 11.

This is the USA's first ever Olympic medal for women's foil. This is an achievement, because Russia is ranked number one in the world!

Erinn and Keeth Smart

Erinn and Keeth Smart have been Peter Westbrook's fencing students for many years.

A Sad Time

Sadly, a few years before the 2008 Olympic Games, both of their parents passed away from illnesses.

Four months before the Games, Keeth went to hospital with a serious illness.

A Positive Attitude

With great strength and a positive attitude, Keeth recovered two months before the Games.

Together, Keeth and Erinn trained hard and qualified for the USA fencing team.

Success!

At the 2008 Beijing Olympic Games Keeth and Erinn won their first silver medals.

Erinn and **Keeth** Email the Author

Email from Erinn Smart

Hi Sharon,

Peter asked me to write to you and let you know why I love fencing. Well, I love fencing for many reasons, but the primary reason is that I learn something new each time I pick up my weapon. There are endless ideas that can be implemented into the sport each time you face an opponent. In one bout, someone can be fearless, passive, agile or maybe aggressive. I find that thrilling each time.

I've attached two pictures of Keeth and myself, but we are not fencing each other. Keeth and I don't fence with the same weapon, so we don't really fence against each other.

Erinn

Author's Email Reply to Erinn Smart

Hi Erinn,

That's perfect. THANK YOU very much! Both you and Keeth have provided a very special insight into what drives and stimulates you within the sport of fencing.

Regards, Sharon

Erinn and Keeth Smart at the 2008 Beijing Olympic Games

Email from Keeth Smart

Hi Sharon,

I love fencing because it is a sport that challenges me physically and mentally. The sport is like a form of physical chess where you have to think two to three moves ahead. I also enjoy the challenges in the sport. I always practise to get better as I never know who might be able to beat me on a given day.

I hope this helps.

Keeth

Erinn and Keeth Smart after winning silver medals at the 2008 Beijing Olympic Games

Keeth fencing at the 2008 Beijing Olympic Games

Author's Email Reply to Keeth Smart

Hello Keeth,

My sincere thanks for sending this email so quickly. The images are amazing and the children will love to read about the success that you and Erinn have so deservedly achieved!

Again, many thanks and all the best to you and your sister for more fencing successes!

Regards, Sharon

Index

Glossary

bout	An individual match in a competition
mesh visor	A protective wire screen that goes in front of the face, but can still be seen through
Paralympics	A comptetitive sports event held after the Olympics for sportspeople with disabilities
pendulum	A weight on the end of a string, wire or bar, that swings from side to side
plastic foam	A thick and dense material made of plastic, used as a protective covering
swash-buckling	Heroic and brave
thrusting sword	A sword with a pointed tip, designed to be poked directly at an opponent
torso	The part of the body that the neck, arms and legs attach to